The Key
Of Insanity 5

The
Continuing
Nightmare

M.Y. Hauger

Introduction

Several days had passed since Myah had escaped that horrible place. For a while, it seemed as though there would be no end to her misery. It was frustrating for Myah because it seemed as though she wasn't able to live a normal life. She would be relocated, and then she would get settled into her new home, only to be moved again.

Once again, Myah found herself at a place that was unknown to her. She hoped that it was the last time that she would have to move. She just wanted to live her life in peace with her son, who was still just a baby during that time.

Myah wished that she could've forgotten what had happened during that horrible moment after she had escaped. She regretted not going back, even though she was told not to. There was still so much about that particular moment that was left unanswered. For Myah, it seemed that not knowing was worse than if she would've known what had happened during that time. She had not heard from anyone since the incident had occurred. She didn't know whether Allen or Albert had escaped or if they were alright. All she knew was that something happened, and it wasn't good. She could still hear the sound of the gunshots as they echoed through her mind. The very thought that someone had gotten hurt or worse left Myah feeling sick to her stomach. She didn't know for sure what it was that had happened, but she suspected that someone had gotten shot.

Myah often wondered whether she had made a mistake by not going back, even though Allen and Albert had both told her to take Michael and leave and not look back. She realized that she needed to keep her son safe, yet she feared that she may have been partially responsible for what may have happened since she decided not to go back.

It wasn't long after Myah had fled when she was met by someone who had then taken her and Michael away from the horrible situation.

Myah hated not hearing from anyone. She wanted to hear from either Allen or Albert. She wanted to know whether they were alright. Because she heard nothing, she feared the possibility that they may not have survived. The very thought of it sickened her, and she lost sleep over it. Myah missed her brother and she didn't want to accept the possibility of him being gone. She hoped to hear from someone soon, so she would know what had happened and if they were okay.

Chapter 1

Myah had recently gotten settled into her new home. She hoped that it would be the final time that she would have to be relocated. She was growing weary of the constant moving around, and she just wanted it to be over. Myah just wanted to move on with her life. She missed all the previous neighborhoods where she lived. Myah sometimes found herself thinking about the people who she had left behind. She missed her friends, including Piper and Albert. She missed Allen, and she often wondered about how he was doing and if he was alright. Myah hated not hearing from him. It seemed like there was no closure, and she found herself wondering if there would ever be closure. She also wondered about how Albert was doing, since he was also involved in that horrible situation.

Everything was strange to Myah, but then again, every place where Myah had been was different from the other places where she had been before. The neighborhood where she was at during that time was completely different, and it was nothing like any of the neighborhoods where she had previously lived.

It was a quiet area and there didn't seem to be very many people close by. There was no yard, only a body of water, and there was also a boardwalk that was nearby.

Myah wasn't sure about her new home because of how different it was. It was a nice, peaceful place where anyone could kick back and relax.

Unfortunately, there was no yard for Michael to play in whenever he would get older. Myah figured that at some point, she could find a place that would be more suitable for them. For the time being, she just wanted to stay where she was at. Myah hated having to start over yet again. Even though the place where she was at was nice, she knew that it would take some time to get used to it. At that point, she just wanted to live a somewhat normal life with her son.

Chapter 2

Since Myah had gotten settled into her new home, she figured that it would be a good idea to find a job. Unfortunately, she also realized that she'd be faced with the problem of trying to find someone to look after Michael while she was at work. Myah didn't know anyone from the area, and she wasn't sure whether there were any daycares nearby. As she thought about it, she began to think about the times when Allen used to tell her that she should consider working online. For a while, she didn't give it much thought because she preferred to work outside the home. With the current situation that she was in, Myah realized that it may have been the solution to her problem. She needed flexibility, and she also realized that it was possibly the best option for her. She would be able to work from home, giving her more time to spend with Michael.

After realizing that an online job was the best option for her with the current situation that she was in, she decided to search the internet for possible work from home opportunities. Many of the jobs were not what she was looking for. Things began to seem hopeless, but then she spotted a job listing that seemed promising. She filled out the application for the job, and then she submitted it. Shortly afterward, a message appeared on the screen that stated that she would be notified by email if she had gotten hired. Myah hoped to hear from the company soon. In the meantime, she took care of Michael, spent time with him, and did other things that kept her occupied throughout the day.

Chapter 3

Later that day, since Michael was asleep, Myah decided to check her emails to see if she had gotten any new messages. She was hoping that there was something regarding the job that she had applied for. As Myah looked through her messages, she noticed that she had received a message from the company. At first, she was nervous about opening the message, but at the same time, she wanted to know whether she had gotten hired. She opened the message and when she read it, she realized that she had gotten hired. She was to start the following day. Myah was happy to see that she had gotten a new job. As she read the message, it was revealed to her what she would be doing. It seemed simple enough, and she was happy that she would be able to spend more time with Michael. Also, she no longer had the dilemma of worrying about finding someone to look after him. She realized that Allen was right, and it was a decision that she should've made sooner.

Chapter 4

The next day, Myah was up bright and early. The first thing she did was check on Michael, who was still asleep. Then she got herself a cup of coffee and a quick bite to eat before she got started with her online job. Myah checked her emails to see if she had received anything new. Sure enough, there was a new message from her manager. Myah read over the message, and then she responded to it shortly afterward. She was confused because she wasn't sure about what she was supposed to do.

After typing in her response, Myah sent it. She was suddenly skeptical about the job and she wondered whether she should search for a different job. Suddenly, she received a new message from the manager with instructions regarding a document that she was supposed to proofread. Myah clicked on the file, and she took a sip of her coffee before she got up to check on Michael. He was still asleep, so Myah went back to her computer and continued her work. She carefully read over the document and made the necessary corrections. Myah then read over it a second time before she sent the revised copy to her manager.

Myah got up to check on Michael, who was awake. She fed him and took care of him, and then she spent time with him until he was about to fall asleep. Afterward, Myah decided to check her emails to make sure she didn't receive another message.

Since Myah didn't receive any more messages, she decided to give Allen a call. It seemed like forever since she had heard from him, and she hoped that he was alright. She took her phone and dialed his number, and then she waited for him to pick it up. There was no response. Myah began to worry, so she tried calling his cell phone, but he didn't respond. Myah began to worry about whether he was the one who had gotten shot. She didn't want to assume the worst, even though she had not heard from him in a while. Myah decided to try back another time, as she hoped that the reason Allen didn't pick up was that he was busy.

Chapter 5

Several days had passed and Myah still heard nothing from Allen or Albert. She worried even more because it wasn't like Allen to not keep in touch. She was about to try to call him when suddenly, she heard a knock on the door. Myah walked over to the door and opened it, but there was no one there. Instead, there was a box that was addressed to Myah. She glanced around before she picked it up, and then she closed the door. Myah inspected the box as she tried to figure out where it may have come from, but there was no return address on it. Myah was hesitant to open the box since she didn't know where it came from. She wasn't expecting any packages, and the only person that she had been in contact with was her manager. As Myah thought about it, she began to wonder if it may have come from them or if it was something from Allen or Albert.

Myah decided to open the box, even though she was somewhat nervous about what was inside it. Myah took a deep breath before she opened the box. Tension built up inside her as she reached into it and pulled out a bag. She was suddenly feeling uncomfortable, and she wasn't sure if she wanted to know what was inside the bag. Myah sighed before she reluctantly looked inside. She was suddenly perplexed, and she reached inside the bag and pulled out the contents of it. It was a shirt that had blood stains on it, and also it had two holes in it. Suddenly, Myah's heart sank, and she felt sick to her stomach as she looked at the shirt. She put it back into the bag because she didn't want to look at it any longer. Part of the mystery of what had happened had finally been solved. It was obvious that at least one person had been shot that day and was possibly killed. Even though Myah knew a little more than what she did before, there were still things that were unanswered. There were still two people who were not accounted for.

Chapter 6

The next day, Myah had a difficult time focusing on her work. All she could think about was that horrible package and the probability that someone had died. She became startled as her phone started ringing. Myah was reluctant to pick it up because she wasn't sure who it may have been. She then answered it, hoping that it may have been someone with answers about Allen's or Albert's whereabouts. Myah sighed before she responded.

"Hello?" she said.

"Hello, Myah. I realize that you probably don't know who it is that you're speaking to. We've only been in contact through emails, however, I felt the need to contact you."

"Is this my manager?" Myah asked.

"Yes."

"Have I done something wrong?"

"No."

"Then, why are you calling?" Myah asked.

"As I said, I felt the need to contact you. Have you been doing alright?" Myah's manager said.

Myah didn't respond.

"Myah, please, don't be afraid. I only want to help. That's what I'm here for." Myah's manager said.

"I'm terribly sorry. I have a lot on my mind." Myah said.

"Perhaps you would like to talk about it."

"I don't even know where to begin. I'm not even sure if it's a good idea to talk about it." Myah said.

"I understand."

"I don't know what to do. I haven't heard from my brother, and I know that something terrible happened. I just don't know if I can talk about it." Myah said.

There was no response.

"Hello?" Myah said.

"I'm just listening."

"I feel so alone."

"You're not alone."

"I am."

"You're not."

"Who do I have? I haven't heard from my brother, and I'm at this place that I know nothing about, and there's nobody around here that I know."

"You have me."

"Thanks, but I barely know you." Myah said.

"I want to help you."

"I'm not sure if there's anything you can do."

"You'd be surprised about what I could do to help." Myah's manager said.

Myah was suddenly perplexed as she continued to listen to the sound of the voice on the other end.

"It's so odd to me." Myah said.

"What is it, Myah?"

"It's your voice."

"What about it?" Myah's manager asked.

"It sounds so familiar. It's so calm and pleasant." Myah said.

"Do you need me to come to your house?"

"I don't think that's necessary. Besides, you don't know where I live."

"Is there anything you need?"

"I really don't know."

"Perhaps you should take a break."

"But I just started a few days ago."

"Yes, I realize that, however I sense that you're going through a rough time."

"You have no idea." Myah said.

"As I said, you should take a break. Give yourself a chance to clear your mind. I'll check back later on to see how you're doing."

"Do you always get so involved in your employees' lives?"

"I try to help whenever I can."

"It seems unusual."

"I take care of my people." Myah's manager said.

Myah then sighed.

"Are you alright?" Myah's manager asked.

"I don't know. Maybe you're right."

"Perhaps you just need some time."

"I won't get fired, will I?"

"Of course not. Why would I fire you? I was the one who suggested that you take a break."

"Right." Myah said.

"Are you sure you don't need me to come over?"

"I don't think that's necessary."

"Very well. If you need to talk, send me an email, and I'll give you a call."

"Thank you." Myah said.

"Take care of yourself."

"Thanks." Myah said.

She then got off the phone.

Chapter 7

After Myah had gotten off the phone with her manager, she just sat there quietly and thought about the conversation that she had. Then she started thinking about what had happened the day before and the package that she had received. At that moment, Myah broke down in tears. She knew that it didn't end well for someone. She felt terrible about what had happened, and she started to blame herself for what had happened. Myah began to wonder if it could have been prevented. She wondered if it would have been any different if she would've never left. Myah sighed and then with tears running down her face, she took her phone and dialed Allen's number. She waited to see if he would pick up the phone, but he didn't. Then she tried his cell phone, but she got no response. Myah shook her head, and then she tried Albert's number. There was no response from him either. Myah sighed, and then she sent an email to her manager. It wasn't long until her phone started to ring. Myah figured that it was probably her manager, so she picked it up.

"Hello?" he said.

"Hey, I'm sorry to bother you, I just needed someone to talk to. I have no one else to talk to except you."

"Myah, listen to me. You're not bothering me. I told you that if you need anything that you can contact me. Did I not?"

"Yes." Myah said.

"Is there something I can do for you?"

"I tried to get a hold of my brother, but there's no answer. As I told you before, I haven't heard from him in days. I'm worried. It's not like him to not keep in touch."

"I see." Myah's manager said.

"There was also another guy, a friend of mine. I tried to contact him, but it's the same thing. There's no response, and I haven't heard from him in a while either. I don't know what to do. I wish I could talk more about the situation, but I'm afraid to."

"Listen to me, Myah. You don't need to be afraid. As I said, I want to help you. I understand if you don't wish to talk about it, however, it may be helpful if I were to know more about it."

"I feel so alone."

"But you're not alone."

"I don't know you. Allen used to always keep in touch with me. Now, I hear nothing from him. I don't know anyone around here."

"Is Allen your brother?" Myah's manager asked.

"Yes."

"The other guy was Albert Hanes. As I told you before, I haven't heard from him either." Myah said.

There was no response.

"There was one other person, but I didn't try to contact him. It's complicated, and I don't wish to talk about it." Myah said.

At that moment, she broke down and wept.

"Would you like for me to come over?" Myah's manager asked.

"No, that's not necessary. Talking on the phone is fine. I just wish that there was someone familiar that I could talk to. Your voice sounds familiar, but it's just not enough. I wish there was someone who was close by that I knew."

"I could come over. It would be no trouble."

"No, but there is one other person whom I wish I could see right now. I've only seen him one time, I mean, I've seen him several times on television, but I saw him once in person. It was like a dream. If only he were here. I'm not sure if I could even talk to him about the situation." Myah said.

"Perhaps you should seek him out. You may be surprised. He may want to help you."

"I'm sure he would, however, I wouldn't even know how to get a hold of him. I heard he's very busy."

"Perhaps he would make time to help you out."

"I feel like we're getting off-topic. The main reason I called is that I haven't heard from my brother." Myah said.

"Right."

"I wish I knew what to do."

"I could take care of it. I'm rather good at figuring things out, although it would be helpful if I knew more about the situation."

"I'm sorry. I'm just not ready to talk about it. It's complicated, and as of yesterday, it has gotten worse." Myah said.

She fought back tears as she thought about the package.

"Listen to me, I know it's difficult, but I promise you that I'll do everything I can to help. You have to believe me. I've noticed that you keep saying that you don't know me, but I'd like for you to trust me." Myah's manager said.

"I just can't talk about it right now." Myah said.

"Very well. I'll try to see what I can do. In the meantime, I want you to try to do something to de-stress. I realize that it's going to be easier said than done, but I'd like for you to try to take your mind off of whatever it is that you're going through. Get out for some fresh air. Take a nap. Do whatever it takes to calm down a bit. As for the situation that you're in, I'll try to take care of it. Remember, if you need to get a hold of me, don't hesitate. I'm more than willing to help."

"Thank you. I do appreciate it, although I'm not sure if there's much that you can do to help."

"I'll do what I can. In the meantime, I want you to take care of yourself, and try to take my advice."

“Alright.” Myah said.

“I’ll check back with you to see how you’re doing.” Myah’s manager said.

“Alright.” Myah said.

She got off the phone shortly afterward.

Chapter 8

After Myah had gotten off the phone, she decided to check on Michael. She took him out of his crib, and then she fed him and took care of him. She spent time with him afterward. No matter how much she wanted to get the awful situation off her mind, it was still in the back of her mind. She just wanted it to stop. She wondered if there would ever be an end to the horrible nightmare.

When Michael was about to fall asleep, Myah put him into the crib. She didn't feel much like doing anything, so she just decided to try to take a nap.

Chapter 9

It was late, and the sky was lit by the moon that shined brightly in the sky. Myah became confused as she glanced around at the surrounding area. Everything was familiar to her, yet she could not remember how she had gotten there. She slowly made her way to the building, and then she glanced around before she went inside. Myah nervously walked toward the ballroom, where everyone else seemed to be headed. When she approached the door, she took a deep breath before she opened the door and stepped inside the room. Since Myah had nobody to dance with, she decided to find a place to sit down. As Myah sat there quietly, her attention was suddenly directed toward the crowd as she noticed something peculiar happening. Suddenly, there was a beam of light that was shining down right in the middle of the crowd. Everyone stepped aside and the Myah suddenly noticed a stranger standing among them where the beam of light was shining. He was dressed in black, and he had a long flowing cape draped across his shoulders. Myah became nervous as she kept her eyes on him. Then suddenly, everything became quiet for a moment. The one who was dressed in black just stood there as he kept his eyes on Myah. Then suddenly, he broke the silence when he started to sing as he held his hand out as he wanted Myah to go to him. Myah didn't want to go to him, and she got up, and she was about to walk away, but then she stopped as she continued to hear the calm soft sound of his voice. Then she turned and looked at him as he continued to sing as he held out his hand. At first Myah tried to resist the sudden urge to go to him, but with every moment that she heard the sound of his voice, she found herself resisting less and less. It was as though she was losing control as she started to gravitate toward him. She continued to move closer and closer to him until she was right there with him. They looked into each other's eyes as he took hold of her hand. Then, he closed his eyes and gave Myah a kiss before the two of them began to dance while everyone watched them quietly. Suddenly, the two of them stopped, and he gazed into Myah's eyes as he gently touched the side of her face. Then he closed his eyes as he gave her another kiss. The two of them looked at one another before Myah hugged him tightly, and then they kissed. They stayed close to one another as the two of them continued to dance. Suddenly, there was a sound of a gunshot followed by screams. Myah became startled and she backed away from him. When she noticed that he had been shot, she screamed loudly.

"Somebody, please! Get help." Myah said.

Her eyes welled up with tears as she watched him fall to the floor.

"No!" she said.

She got down beside him and took him into her arms as she started to cry. As he looked at her, he reached up and touched her face, and then she spoke softly to her.

"Don't worry, my dear. I will see to it that nothing separates us again. We'll be together forever. Nothing will ever keep us apart." he said.

He struggled as he sat up. Myah could see that he was in pain. He looked into her eyes for a moment, and then he closed his eyes as he gave Myah a kiss. They hugged one another tightly and suddenly, Myah felt his teeth sink into her. She gasped and then she opened her eyes. As she glanced around, she suddenly noticed that she was in her room on her bed. It was then that she realized that it was a nightmare. Myah cupped her hands to her face as she started to cry. She wasn't sure about how much more she could take. Myah just wanted the never-ending nightmare to come to a stop. She wiped the tears from her face before she got up from her bed. Then she left her room to check on Michael, who was still asleep. Since he wasn't awake, Myah decided to go back to her room. As she sat down on the bed, she broke down in tears. It seemed like there was no end to the reminders of what had happened and how there was one whose life had been cut short. Even though Myah was still tired, she wasn't sure if she even wanted to go back to sleep. She was afraid that she would be trapped once again in a horrible nightmare that would remind her of what had happened. Every moment of her life became like a prison as she was continually reminded of the one who had gotten shot.

Chapter 10

Two days had passed since Myah had talked to her manager. She was debating whether she wanted to go outside and take a walk. She was a bit nervous about going out since she was still unfamiliar with the area, and she didn't know anyone from the area. Myah was about to take Michael out of the crib when she heard a knock on the door. She sighed before she walked over to the door and answered it. Myah became nervous when she spotted another package. She wasn't sure whether she wanted to pick it up. Nevertheless, she reluctantly took it inside. Myah took it to the coffee table and put it down before she checked on Michael, who had fallen asleep. She sighed before she made her way back into the living room and sat down. Then she grabbed the box, and she reluctantly opened it and looked inside it. Her heart sank as she noticed the contents of the box. It was the belongings of the one who had gotten shot. There was also an envelope that contained a large sum of money. Myah put the box back down on the coffee table before she cupped her hands to her face as she started to cry. She wasn't sure how much more she could take. She just wanted the nightmare to be over, but it seemed like it would never end. As she sat there, she was taken back to when she was told that she would never forget him and that he would be in all her thoughts and all her dreams. It was then that she realized that her troubles were far from over, and she would forever be tormented by him even though he was not there.

Chapter 11

That night, Myah found it difficult to rest. All she could think about were the things that were in the box that she had received that day. She sighed before she got up because she decided to check on Michael. She left her room and went into his room and looked into his crib. He was sound asleep, and Myah sighed before she went back to her room and sat down on her bed. She glanced over at the phone that was in her room before she picked it up and dialed Allen's number. There was no answer, so she dialed his cell phone number, but there was no response. She tried to call Albert, but he didn't respond either. She hung up the phone, and she looked at it for a moment because she was tempted to call her manager. Myah decided not to call him because she didn't want to bother him late in the night.

As time went on, Myah grew tired and eventually, she drifted off to sleep, but unfortunately, it wasn't a restful night for her. While she was asleep, Myah was tormented by the things that had happened before that fateful day when she had managed to escape. It was like she was reliving it all over again. Then suddenly everything became still and it became dark. Myah found herself in her room. Suddenly, the clock struck midnight. She was confused because she thought for sure that it was later than that. There was a sudden uneasiness that overtook her. Myah became startled as there was a crack of thunder and then the lightning flashed through the sky. The wind picked up, and then the window blew open. Suddenly, the bedroom door came open and then there was a strange fog. As it cleared, Myah became horrified as she noticed someone standing there. It was the one who had been shot. He was dressed as he was before, all dressed in black, and he wore a long flowing cape. He was silent as he stood there and stared at Myah. Tension rose inside Myah as she wondered if she was seeing things, or if it was a ghost. She was terrified, and she just wanted him to go away. He kept his eyes on Myah as he took a few steps forward, as he entered the room. Then he held his hand out to her, letting her know that he wanted her to come to him. Myah's heart raced as she pulled the blanket over her head because she didn't want to see him. Then suddenly, she heard the calm, soft sound of his voice as he started to sing. As Myah listened to the sound of his voice, she suddenly found herself wanting to get up and move toward him. Myah got out from under the blanket, and then she got up off the bed. They kept their eyes on one another as Myah moved toward him as he continued to sing. When she approached him, she nervously reached up and touched the side of his face. She felt a sudden chill as he put his arms around her. They both closed their eyes as they kissed. His lips were as cold as ice, and it caused her to shiver. He looked into her eyes for a moment before he kissed her again. Myah trembled as she looked at him. Suddenly, two wounds appeared, and he started to bleed. He could see that she was becoming more nervous, so he took hold of her and held her tighter as he kissed her, letting her know that he had no intention of letting her go. Tension rose inside Myah as he held her even tighter. Then, suddenly, she felt his teeth sink into her. At that very moment, the phone rang and Myah opened her eyes before she sat up on her bed. It was then that she realized that it was all just a bad dream, but the phone was still ringing. At first, she was hesitant to pick it up. The phone continued to ring until Myah decided to pick it up.

"Hello?" Myah said.

"Myah? I know it's late, but I wanted to see how you were doing. I wanted to make sure you were alright." Myah's manager said.

"I don't know. I just woke up."

"I'm sorry."

"No, it's okay, really. Actually, I'm glad you woke me up. I was having a nightmare and thanks to you, it's over now. Thank you."

"I'm sorry to hear that you're having a rough night. Do you need to talk about it?" Myah's manager said.

Myah hesitated for a moment, and then she spoke.

"Do you remember when I told you that there was a person who I didn't want to talk about?" she said.

"Yes."

"The nightmare was about him. He came back and he was a vampire. It's not the first time I've had dreams like this about him, and they always feel so real. I don't know why, but for some reason, he had a thing with vampires. He liked watching vampire movies."

"Vampires?"

"Yeah." Myah said.

"I see."

"It's a complicated situation. You see, I got mixed up with this guy. At first, it wasn't by choice, but he was persistent and with time, he kind of grew on me, but he had problems. There was something wrong with him. I don't know what it was, but he was an emotional mess." Myah said.

"You got mixed up with this guy, and now you're having nightmares about him."

"Yes. As I said, he had problems. He once told me that I would never forget him. He said that he'd be in all my thoughts and my every dream. The truth is, he was right. Unfortunately, he did some things that caused me to become terrified of him. The thing is, I still care about him. I fell in love with him. I still love him and I miss him."

"Where is he now?" Myah's manager asked.

At that moment, Myah broke down and wept.

"I'm very sorry. Is there anything I can do to help you?" Myah's manager asked.

"No, I don't think there is. There's nothing that can be done. I just don't know how much more I can take. Things keep happening, and it just seems like the nightmare won't end."

"Were you planning to be with him?"

"I don't know. He was acting kind of scary toward the end. I feel like he needed help."

"Do you want me to try to find him?" Myah's manager asked.

"You can't."

"Why not?"

"You just can't." Myah said.

"I'm sorry. I know that this doesn't change the situation, but if there's anything that you need, I'll be more than willing to help you. Don't hesitate to ask. That's why I'm here."

"Sometimes I wish it would just go away. I wish I could just forget about him and move on with my life."

"Is that really what you want?" Myah's manager asked.

"I don't know. Ever since he entered my life, it's been nothing but chaos. It doesn't really matter because it's not like I'll ever forget. He's made it clear that I will never forget, and it seems that he was right."

"I'm truly sorry."

"I'm not even sure if I can go back to sleep. I'm almost afraid to. I don't have another nightmare." Myah said.

For a moment, the other end was silent, but then Myah's manager spoke.

"Myah, I want you to do something for me."

"What is it?" Myah asked.

"I want you to listen to the sound of my voice. I want you to focus on it, and I want you to try to clear your mind. I know that it's difficult, but I need you to concentrate on the sound of my voice." Myah's manager said.

At that moment, Myah suddenly felt less tense. She continued to listen to the sound of her manager's voice as he spoke to her. Then he started to sing, and she started to relax. As time went on, she felt more relaxed until finally, she drifted off to sleep.

Chapter 12

Several days had passed since Myah had received the second package. She tried to continue with her life, and that included the work that she needed to do. Myah was still struggling with the things that had been happening. She just wanted it to end. Then suddenly, she heard a knock on the door. After receiving the last two packages, Myah was reluctant to see what was out there. Then she heard another knock on the door. She didn't want to answer it. Instead, she decided to check on Michael, who was asleep during that time. When Myah walked back out to the living room, she spotted something on the floor. As she approached it, she realized that it was an envelope that was addressed to her. She was puzzled because she didn't hear the door open or close. Myah sighed before she reluctantly picked it up. There was no return address on it, so there was no way of knowing where it came from. Even though Myah had a feeling she would regret it, she decided to open the envelope anyway. She walked over to the sofa, and then she sat down before she carefully opened it. She then pulled out a photograph of a baby boy who looked identical to Michael. Myah knew that the baby in the photograph wasn't her son because it appeared to be from a different time period. When Myah turned the photo to look at the back of it, she noticed that it was from ten years ago. Myah put the photo down, and then she pulled another one out of the envelope. She noticed right away that it was another baby boy who looked exactly like her son, but she knew that it wasn't him because it appeared to be an even older photo than the last one. Myah put the photograph down with the other one, and then she pulled out one more photo. That time, it was a collage and there were three photos in it. All three of them were baby boys who looked like Michael, but they were from different time periods. One of the photos was Michael, but the other two were the other babies who looked like Michael. At that moment, chills ran down Myah's spine as she was taken back to a conversation that she had not long ago. As she studied each photo in the collage, she noticed that all three babies were spitting images of one another. At that moment, Myah's heart sank, and she started to feel sick to her stomach. Even though she didn't know the identity of the baby picture from ten years ago, she had a feeling that she did know the identity of the baby who was in the older photograph. Her heart sank deeper because she knew that there was no denying it because it was right in front of her face, and she could no longer run from the truth.

Chapter 13

Two days had passed since Myah had received the envelope. Once again, she found herself unable to focus on her work. Myah sighed, and then she sent a message to her manager. It was shortly afterward when the phone rang. Since she figured that it was probably him, she picked it up.

"Hello?" Myah said.

"Hello, Myah. I received your message. What do you need to talk about?"

"I'm terribly sorry. I just don't think I can do this." Myah said.

Suddenly, there was an awkward silence. It wasn't long after that when she heard a knock on the door. Myah wasn't sure whether she should answer it.

"Myah?"

"When Myah realized that the voice was familiar, she walked over to the door and answered it. She was suddenly shocked when she saw who it was that was standing at the door.

"May I come in?" he asked.

Myah remained speechless as she looked at who was standing in front of her.

"You messaged me because you needed to talk. Am I right?" he said.

"You're my manager?" Myah said.

“Yes.”

“But you’re…” Myah said.

They both became silent for a moment. Myah stepped aside as she let him inside. Myah then closed the door.

“I should’ve known it was you. That’s why your voice sounded so familiar.” Myah said.

As she looked at him, she noticed the unhappy expression on his face.

“Your majesty, I’m really sorry to bother you.” Myah said.

“First off, call me Endymion. Secondly, you need to stop thinking that you’re bothering me. I told you already that you’re not bothering me. I’ve made it clear that I want to help.”

“Right. I just wasn’t expecting it. As I was saying on the phone, I don’t know if I can do this.” Myah said.

With an unhappy expression on his face, Endymion responded.

"How about we sit down." he said.

They both walked over to the sofa and sat down.

"Now, talk to me." Endymion said.

"As you know, I've been dealing with some things. I told you a little about it, but I didn't tell you everything."

"Right. I believe the last thing you told me was that you got yourself mixed up in a difficult situation."

"Yes, but that's not the entire story."

"Tell me more." Endymion said.

"As I told you before, I feel like something terrible has happened. There were three other people involved, aside from my son and me. I haven't heard from any of them. One of those people was my brother."

"Keep talking."

"I really don't know much about it because I took my son and ran. That's what they told me to do. As I fled, I heard two gunshots. I don't know if any of the other people had survived. I'm almost certain that one of them didn't." Myah said.

At that moment, she broke down in tears.

"Recently, I received three strange packages. It seemed to be evidence that one of them had been killed. It was disturbing, and I wish that I would've never opened any of them." Myah said.

"May I see them?" Endymion asked.

Myah didn't respond.

"It's okay. I get it. I realize that it's difficult, but I want to help." Endymion said.

Myah was hesitant for a moment, but then she got up and walked to the dining room where the packages were. She picked them up, and took them to the living room. Then she handed them to Endymion before she sat down. Endymion sat the boxes down on the coffee table, and then he took the envelope and opened it before he pulled the photos out of it. Myah could see that Endymion was fighting back tears as he studied each photograph closely. He looked at the collage, studying each photo that was on it, and then he put it down. When he looked at the photo that was from ten years ago, he managed to smile, and then he put the photograph down. Then he looked at the older photograph, and he found himself fighting back tears again.

"You've been wondering about this particular photograph and the identity of the child in it. I can put your doubts and uncertainties to rest. This child was the man who you were involved with." Endymion said.

"How did you know?"

"I just know. As for him, I know him."

"Then he was telling the truth."

"About your son?"

"Yes."

"Yes. How could you not see it? I could see it right away. He's the spitting image of him. That, I know for a fact." Endymion said.

"What about the other baby?" Myah asked.

Endymion didn't respond. He then sighed as he opened one of the boxes. It was the one that contained the belongings. He glanced at Myah, and then he continued to look through his things."

"How serious were the two of you?" Endymion asked.

"It was complicated. As I said before, I think there was something wrong with him. At times, he was so unpredictable, sometimes he was scary." Myah said.

Endymion closed the box and then set it aside. Then he took the other box and opened it. He seemed unhappy as he looked inside the box. He took the bag out of it, and then he glanced at Myah before he opened the bag and took the shirt out of it. As Endymion looked at the blood stained shirt, his eyes filled with tears.

"Why?" Endymion said.

Then he sighed, and he shook his head before he put the shirt back into the bag. Afterward, he cupped his hands to his face as he broke down and wept.

"I don't know what to do. He was the father of my son, and now, he's..." Myah said.

Endymion looked at her with tears running down his face.

"Someone had abandoned him. He was left on my porch, so I took him in. As for the man, he showed up shortly afterward. He told me that he was the baby's father. I didn't want to believe him, even though, deep down, I kind of knew it was true. It's just as you said. He looks just like him." Myah said.

Endymion then hugged Myah as tears ran down his face.

"I'm so sorry, Myah. Endymion said.

"I was expecting a baby, but things went wrong, and I think I may have lost it."

"You haven't lost it, Myah, in fact, you're carrying two of them."

"What?"

"It's true. You're carrying twins." Endymion said.

At that moment, Myah's eyes welled up with tears.

"What am I going to do? Their father is dead." Myah said.

Endymion got choked up as he looked at her.

"Listen to me, Myah. I promise you that you will not have to go through this alone. I will help you. I will take care of you, Michael, and the ones you are carrying." Endymion said.

"How did you know that my son's name is Michael?" Myah asked.

Endymion didn't respond.

"I'm sorry." Myah said.

"There's no need to apologize. This is a difficult time for us. I have to go for a moment, but I will return." Endymion said.

He and Myah looked at one another before Endymion gave her a hug.

"I'll be back, I promise." he said.

Endymion then stood up, and he headed toward the door. He looked at her for a moment before he quietly walked out the door.

Chapter 14

It was several hours later when Endymion returned. As Myah left him inside, she could see the pain that was in his eyes.

"I'm very sorry. I needed time to myself." Endymion said.

"You don't need to apologize."

"I understand that it's a difficult situation for you, but it's also painful for me." Endymion said.

He then glanced toward Michael's room before he started walking in that direction. When he approached the crib, he looked inside it before he picked Michael up.

"As I said, you won't have to go through this alone. We're in this together, and I'll help you through it." Endymion said.

"I appreciate it." Myah said.

Endymion then looked at Michael. He fought back tears as he spoke softly to him. He then gave him a kiss on the forehead before he started to sing to him. Myah watched him closely as he interacted with her son. Then Endymion walked over to Myah and gave the baby to her, and she took care of him.

"I want to help you in every way possible. I can't promise you that I can be here all the time because there are many others that I must take care of. I'll try to be here as often as I can." Endymion said.

"I understand. I've heard that you are a busy person."

"I truly wish I could be here all the time, especially with all that's been going on. I'll provide the needs of you and your family. It's the least I can do for you. I wish I could do more."

"But you've done so much already."

"But it's not enough. I'm not sure that it ever will be." Endymion said.

"But it's not your responsibility."

"I feel that it is." Endymion said.

When he saw that Myah had finished taking care of Michael, he took him, and then he started speaking softly to him before he started singing to him until he eventually fell asleep. Then Endymion took Michael to his crib and carefully put him into it. He looked at Myah with a sorrowful expression on his face as he walked over to her. Then they both sat down on the sofa. Myah broke down in tears, and then Endymion hugged her tightly as she wept. They stayed there for most of the day. Myah ended up falling asleep in Endymion's strong embrace. As he sat there, he thought about what she told him about having nightmares about the one who had been shot. He decided to give her a good dream in hopes of helping her to get a good night's sleep. Endymion was unable to fall asleep. Since he stayed awake, he got up whenever Michael woke up, and he took care of him so that Myah could get some rest. There were also times during the night when Endymion broke down and wept. He took notice of a flower pot that had no flowers in it. He got up and he walked over to it. As he looked into it, a tear trickled down his face and fell into the flower pot, and it caused a purple crystallized flower to come up out of the soil and bloom. Endymion sighed, and then he walked back over to the sofa and sat down. It was not a restful night for him as he thought about the one who had been shot.

Chapter 15

The next morning, Myah woke up to Endymion preparing breakfast. She glanced over at Michael, who was still asleep.

"I already took care of him while you were still asleep. I wasn't able to sleep, so I took care of him through the night." Endymion said.

"You should have woken me up." Myah said.

"It's not a big deal. Besides, you needed to get some rest. I'm used to not getting much sleep."

"You were thinking about him."

"Yes. I will have to go after a bit, but I will return. I won't be able to stay for very long. Unfortunately, I'm going to have to look for him so that I can lay him to rest." Endymion said.

Myah could see that Endymion was fighting back tears. He sighed and then he finished preparing breakfast. He served Myah and then he sat down.

"Aren't you going to eat?" Myah asked.

"I'm afraid that I don't have an appetite. You, on the other hand, need to eat." Endymion said.

Myah was about to sit down when she spotted the flower that was in the flower pot.

"Where did that come from?" Myah asked.

She then walked over to it, so she could get a closer look at it.

"That has to be one of the most beautiful flowers I have ever seen. Where did it come from?" Myah said.

"It came from me. They usually come up when my tears fall to the ground whenever I mourn." Endymion said.

Myah's heart sank.

"I'm so sorry."

"It's alright. I noticed the flower pot had no flower in it, so I walked over to it and one of my tears fell into it. That's how the flower got there." Endymion said.

"I wish you didn't have to go."

"I know, but I have to. I have so much to do. I will come back to drop off some things, but afterward, I must find him. I also plan to search for the two who are missing."

"You would do that?"

"Of course. Unfortunately, you do realize that if I find out that they were responsible for his death, they will have to go to prison." Endymion said.

"Yes, I understand."

"I hope that you won't hold it against me. I hate murder and I have no tolerance for it. If he had been the one who pulled the trigger, the consequence would be the same for him as well. Unfortunately, the situation is a bit more complicated since it's personal and very painful for me." Endymion said.

He then stood up.

"I have to go. As I said, I'll be back." he said.

Then he quietly left Myah's house.

Chapter 16

It was two hours later when Endymion returned, and he had food, diapers, and other things that Myah would need. He glanced at Myah before she started putting things away.

"I brought some food and other things for you." Endymion said.

"Thank you." Myah said.

After Endymion put everything away, he walked over to Michael and checked on him to see how he was doing. He was awake, so Endymion picked him up.

"Thank you. I could've gotten him." Myah said.

"It's no big deal. I don't mind." Endymion said.

He started to speak to Michael, who smiled and cooed as he looked at him. It was a bittersweet moment for Myah as she watched him interact with her son.

"He really seems to like you." Myah said.

Endymion said nothing as he glanced at her.

"He looks more and more like him as time goes on. Sometimes, it's so hard for me. Every time I close my eyes, I see his face. I hear the sound of his voice." Myah said.

Endymion had a sorrowful expression on his face as he looked at Myah.

"Would it be easier if I took him for a few days?" he asked.

"No. I would miss him. Besides, he's all that I have left." Myah said.

"I'm sorry. It was just a suggestion."

"You don't need to apologize. I know that you were just trying to help." Myah said.

She and Endymion walked over to the sofa and sat down.

"He was right whenever he said that I would never forget him." Myah said.

"I'd imagine that it would be rather hard to forget about him whenever you have his son who looks like him. Also, more than likely, the ones you're carrying will probably look like him as well." Endymion said.

"What am I going to do?"

"I already told you that you will not have to go through it alone. Even though I can't be here all the time, I'll try to be here as much as possible."

"Endymion?"

"Yes?"

"Please, don't go." Myah said.

"I'm sorry, but I must. I have to find him." Endymion said.

"I understand. I just wish that you didn't have to go."

"I can stay for a little, but this is something that needs to be done."

"Endymion?"

"Yes?"

"Thank you for coming."

"I told you that I wanted to help you."

"Thank you for helping out with Michael. I really do appreciate it."

"It's no problem."

"I like how you interact with him. He used to speak to him and sing to him, just as you do." Myah said.

Endymion glanced over at her with a sorrowful expression on his face.

"It's been nice having you around, even if it hasn't been for very long. It's not so lonely when you're here." Myah said.

Endymion glanced down at Michael, who was about to fall asleep. He stood up and took him to his crib and put him into it. Then he made his way back into the living room. Myah stood up, and then she made her way over to him. They looked at one another for a moment before Myah gave him a hug.

"I really should soon get going. I have things that I need to do. I want you to take care of yourself in the meantime. I will come back." Endymion said.

"Thank you." Myah said.

"You're welcome." Endymion said.

He then left Myah's home.

Chapter 17

It was later in the day when Endymion had returned, and he had the boy with him that Myah had seen at the party when she lived near the village.

"You've come back." Myah said.

"I told you that I would. I hope you don't mind that I brought him with me." Endymion said.

"No, I don't mind. I think I remember him from the party."

"Yes." Endymion said.

The child that was with him remained silent as he looked at Myah nervously.

"You don't need to be nervous, son." Endymion said.

The boy remained quiet as he looked at Endymion, and then he quietly walked away.

"He gets a little shy at times. When he gets to know people, he opens up more." Endymion said.

"He seems like a sweet kid." Myah said.

"Yes, he's a very good kid. Unfortunately, the world hasn't always been kind to him. He deserves so much better."

"I'm so sorry." Myah said.

As the two of them made their way to the sofa, they noticed the boy holding Michael.

"Aww." Myah said.

"Yes, he's such a good child. He's very helpful. He often helps with his siblings."

"How many siblings does he have?" Myah asked.

"Several."

"Oh."

"It's a long story." Endymion said.

Myah smiled as she looked at the child, but then suddenly her smile went away as she fought back tears.

"I see him everywhere. Even in that child. Why?" Myah said.

She then looked at Endymion as her eyes welled up with tears.

"Why does he look like him?" Myah asked.

Endymion frowned as he glanced at Myah and looked at the boy.

"Who is she talking about?" the boy asked.

"Please, don't worry about it, my son." Endymion said.

His eyes welled up with tears as he turned his face.

"Did I do something wrong?" the boy asked.

Endymion's heart sank as he looked at the child.

"Of course not." Endymion said.

He made his way over to the child, sat down beside him, and then he gave him a hug. As Endymion closed his eyes, a tear trickled down his face. Then he looked at Myah with a sorrowful expression on his face before he spoke.

"Perhaps we should go. I wasn't thinking when I came here with him. I'm very sorry." Endymion said.

"No, Endymion. Please, don't go, and you don't need to apologize. I can see he means a lot to you."

"He means the world to me, and more." Endymion said.

He then stood up.

"I should probably start dinner. We try not to eat late, although, at times, it's unavoidable." Endymion said.

"You don't need to do that." Myah said.

"I insist." Endymion said.

He then got up and washed his hands before he started to prepare dinner.

"At some point, I'll have to go back and continue my search.

Unfortunately, I haven't found anything yet. I returned because I wanted to see how you were doing." Endymion said.

"Can you at least stay with me through the night?" Myah asked.

Endymion said nothing as he glanced at her.

"Nights are difficult for me. Most of the time, I'm afraid to go to sleep because I just know that I'll end up having another nightmare about him." Myah said.

Endymion remained silent as he looked at Myah.

"Please, stay." Myah said.

"I don't know if I should. I need to find him. Besides, did you not want me to find your brother?"

"Yes, of course." Myah said.

Endymion kept busy as he continued to prepare dinner. When it was ready, he served everyone before he served himself. He gave thanks before they started to eat.

"I want to thank you for this. It's very good, and you really didn't have to go to all that trouble." Myah said.

"It wasn't any trouble." Endymion said.

After dinner, Endymion and the boy washed the dishes and cleaned the table while Myah checked on Michael, who was awake. She took care of him while Endymion and the boy kept busy in the kitchen. Afterward, everyone went into the living room. Endymion and Myah sat down. Then, the boy made his way over to Myah. She could tell that he wanted to hold Michael, so she gave him to him, and then the boy sat down.

Endymion stayed with Myah for several hours. He helped Myah get Michael ready for bed before he took the boy and left. Myah was sad that Endymion had decided to leave.

"I'll be back to check to see how you're doing." Endymion said.

He then took the boy and left.

Chapter 18

Several hours had passed, and Myah was unable to sleep. She found herself missing Endymion, and she was also afraid to fall asleep because she didn't want to have a nightmare. As she rested on the bed, she heard a knock on the door, so she got up and answered it.

"Endymion?" Myah said.

"I see that you're having difficulty going to sleep. Perhaps I could help you with that."

"Please, come in." Myah said.

Endymion stepped inside, and then he closed the door.

"I want to apologize for earlier. It's not that I don't want to help you. I've made it clear on several occasions that I do want to help you. You must understand the importance of me finding him, so he can be laid to rest." Endymion said.

He fought back tears as he looked at Myah.

"You have no idea how difficult this is for me." Endymion said.

His eyes welled up with tears as he looked down at the floor. Myah took hold of Endymion's hand, and then she took him into the living room, where they sat down on the sofa. She looked at him for a moment before she hugged him. Tears ran down Endymion's face as he rested against Myah who hugged him even tighter. She was suddenly taken back to similar moments that took place not so long ago. Endymion knew what

Myah was thinking about, and his heart sank even deeper. Then he sat up, and then he looked into her eyes as he spoke.

"Perhaps I should help you to get some rest." Endymion said.

Myah got up, and then she took hold of Endymion's hand before he stood up. They both went to Myah's room and then Myah sat down on the bed. Endymion hesitated for a moment before he sat down with her. Myah reached up and touched the side of Endymion's face, and then Endymion took hold of her hand as he looked into her eyes and began to sing. As he sang to Myah, she began to feel relaxed, but then she was suddenly reminded of the dreams she had of the one who was dressed in black sang to her. With a sorrowful expression on his face, Endymion stopped singing. Then he sighed, and he closed his eyes before he started to sing again until Myah had fallen asleep. Endymion fought back tears as he looked at Myah, and then he got up and left the room to check on Michael, who was awake. Endymion took care of him, and he spent time with him. He fought back tears as he looked at the baby and was taken back to a time years ago when he came to a baby during the night to comfort and take care of him. When Michael was about to fall asleep, Endymion put him back into his crib, and then he made his way over to the sofa and sat down. He cupped his hands to his face as he broke down and wept. Then, with a heavy heart, Endymion left, so he could be alone in his grief.

Chapter 19

Several hours had passed, and Endymion returned to where he had been staying, where he was taking care of the boy and his siblings. When he got there, he glanced at Officer Aaron before he spoke.

"You can go home to your family now. I'll see you in the morning." Endymion said.

Officer Aaron nodded before he left. Then Endymion sighed before he went upstairs to check on the boy and his siblings. First, he checked on the youngest ones, who were asleep. Then he checked on the boy's other sibling, who was also asleep. Lastly, he went into the boy's room to see how he was doing. Endymion quietly left the room and went back down the stairs and sat down on the sofa. He sighed as he sat there, and then he cupped his hands to his face as he tried to fight back tears. Suddenly, he sensed someone else's presence and when he looked up, he noticed the boy standing in front of him with an expression of concern on his face. The boy remained quiet as he gave Endymion a hug. At that moment, Endymion broke down in tears as he hugged him.

"I love you, my son. I feel like I can't say it enough. I love you." Endymion said.

"I love you too." the boy said.

Then he looked Endymion in the eyes before he spoke.

"What's the matter? Why are you so sad?" he asked.

"I can't tell you, not now, my son." Endymion said.

The boy gave Endymion another hug.

"You should be in bed, my son. Growing boys need their rest." Endymion said.

"So do grown men." the boy said.

"I'll be alright. You, on the other hand, should go back upstairs to your room."

"Can I stay down here with you?" the boy asked.

"Very well." Endymion said.

The boy sat down on the sofa with Endymion. Then he started to sing as he sat there beside Endymion, who just looked at him for a moment before he started to sing. As they harmonized, both of them began to feel tired until eventually, they had both fallen asleep.

Chapter 20

The next morning, Myah woke up and discovered that Endymion wasn't there. She got up from her bed and checked on Michael, who was still asleep. Then she went out to the living room, but he wasn't there either. Just then, there was a knock on the door. Without hesitation, Myah went to the door and answered it.

"Hello, Myah." Endymion said.

"Hi."

"How did you sleep?"

"I slept alright." Myah said.

She then stepped aside.

"Please, come in." Myah said.

Endymion stepped inside, and then he closed the door behind him.

"I wanted to see how you're doing. I plan to continue my search today." Endymion said.

At that moment, Myah gave Endymion a hug.

"I wish it was over." she said.

Endymion fought back tears as he spoke.

"So do I." he said.

"I'm going to miss you." Myah said.

Endymion looked at Myah nervously.

"How about I fix breakfast for you before I go?" he said.

"You don't need to do that."

"It's fine, really." Endymion said.

Without hesitation, he washed his hands before he started to prepare breakfast while Myah checked on Michael, who was still asleep. When breakfast was ready, Endymion served Myah, and then he got breakfast for himself before he sat down and gave thanks.

"So, how are you doing this morning?" Myah asked.

"As well as expected. How are you doing?"

"I've been better." Myah said.

"They say it gets easier with time, but the thing is, it never goes away completely. Unfortunately, it leaves a scar, as most deep wounds would."

"I wish it wouldn't have been so complicated. Maybe if things would've been different, certain things could've been avoided."

"Then again, it could've ended up being something else." Endymion said.

Then he looked at Myah as he continued to speak.

"I don't want you to blame yourself for what happened to him. I understand that it was a difficult situation, and the best thing we can do is do our best to get through it."

"Sometimes I do feel like it was my fault. Had I never ran, maybe he would've never gotten shot."

"You don't know that. For one thing, you don't know what happened. We can make guesses about it, but with so little to go on, that's all it would be. A guess. Also, you did the right thing because you have to make sure the child is kept safe. Staying there would've never guaranteed that it wouldn't have happened. It may have made things worse for you if you would've seen it happen. That wouldn't be a good thing, besides, the last thing you would want to do is put the child in danger." Endymion said.

"I understand what you're saying. I just wish that it could've been avoided."

"So do I. As I said, I plan to continue my search. Also, I want answers, even if they're answers that we don't want to hear."

"I understand." Myah said.

After breakfast, Endymion cleaned everything up. Afterward, he took care of Michael and spent time with him until he went back to sleep. Then he put him back into his crib.

"I think I'm going to head out. I'll keep in touch. If I find anything out, I'll let you know." Endymion said.

"Okay. Be careful."

"I will." Endymion said.

They both walked over to the door. As Endymion was about to open the door, Myah stopped him. They looked at one another for a moment, before Myah gave him a kiss. Endymion suddenly seemed sorrowful as he looked into Myah's eyes.

"I should go." he said.

"Will you be back soon?" Myah asked.

Endymion frowned.

"I have to find him." he said.

He then turned, opened the door, and left.

Chapter 21

Endymion fought back tears, and his heart sank deeper and deeper as he continued to walk away. He cared about both Myah and Michael, and he wanted to help them out as much as possible, but he didn't like where things were going at that time. Endymion knew that she was seeing the one who had gotten shot every time she looked at him, and it made him feel uncomfortable. Also, he felt that it was much too soon, and he didn't want to become a rebound, only to have his heart broken later on. Endymion decided that it was best to focus on continuing his search and get to the bottom of what had happened during that horrible incident. With that, Endymion vanished from where he was, so he could return to the area where he had begun his search.

Chapter 22

Several days had passed since Endymion had left Myah's home, and she decided to take Michael and go out and take a walk. It would be the first time she would ever leave her home. She was a bit nervous about it, but at the same time, she hoped it would help to take her mind off of everything that had been going on. She was also missing Endymion at that point, and she wanted to try to take her mind off of him as well.

Myah took Michael, and she fed him and changed him before she put him into the stroller before she left her home. It was a quiet afternoon. Everything seemed calm and still. There didn't seem to be many people outside during that time.

As Myah continued to walk, she spotted what appeared to be a small village with several small shops. It was the first time that Myah had been to the area, and it seemed interesting, so she decided to check it out. She continued to walk in the direction of the small village and when she got there, she glanced around for a moment before she continued to walk. The only people who were out were a few who were sitting on their porches. As Myah continued to walk, she glanced at one of the small shops. She wanted to go inside, and she was about to head toward it when she caught a glimpse of someone walking on the lane that was behind the shop. It was someone familiar.

"No." she thought to herself.

Without hesitation, she found a place to hide.

"It couldn't be." she thought to herself.

As Myah remained hidden, she watched the familiar person closely. She wasn't sure whether her eyes were playing tricks on her or she was actually seeing who she thought she was seeing. It couldn't have been who she thought it was. All evidence pointed to the probability that he was dead. Myah had to be sure, so she continued to watch him closely, hoping that he wouldn't know that she was there. Suddenly, he started coming toward the direction where she was hiding. As he moved closer, Myah realized that it actually was who she thought it was. There he was, Jayden Williams, as plain as day, in the same area where Myah was, and he appeared as though he was searching for something or someone. As he continued to glance around, he had an unhappy expression on his face, and it seemed as though he was in pain. There was no doubt he somehow knew that she was in the area. Myah began to worry about the possibility of Jayden knowing where she lived. Although she cared about him, and she was relieved that he wasn't dead, she didn't like the idea of him being so close. The last thing that Myah wanted was for him to find her. Myah feared that if he found her, he would make her miserable again. There would also be the possibility of him seeking revenge on her for running away. She feared the possibility of him holding her responsible for whatever had happened on that horrible day, giving him more reason to seek revenge on her. Myah didn't want to relive the horrible nightmare that she had experienced not long ago. She didn't want to be tormented by him, nor could she stand the thought of the constant yelling that she had to endure while she was imprisoned by him. She didn't want Jayden to make her miserable again. Myah knew that she had to do something. She remained hidden as she hoped that he wouldn't spot her. Myah watched him closely as he moved on. He continued to glance around as he walked through the village.

Then, he headed toward the shop. When he approached it, he glanced around before he went inside. Myah thought it was the perfect opportunity to quickly get back to her home before Jayden exited the shop. Without hesitation, Myah left her hiding spot and headed toward her home as quickly as possible, as she hoped to not get captured by Jayden.

Chapter 23

Several days had passed since Myah had seen Jayden. For a while, she was afraid to go back outside because she didn't know if Jayden was still around. She found it strange because any other time, he would've found her, but this time seemed to be different. Myah began to wonder if Jayden may have finally given up and left the area. She liked the idea of him finally leaving her alone so that she could move on with her life, so she could take care of her family. Myah felt that she could also move on with her life knowing that Jayden was still alive, even though she didn't want him there with her.

Even though the mystery had been solved about Jayden, there were still things that were unanswered. Myah still had not heard anything from Albert or Allen, nor had she heard from Endymion. She didn't know whether Allen and Albert had also been shot or if they were okay. If they were alright, why were they not contacting her? There were still things about the situation that didn't make sense. Myah wanted to believe that they were both alright, even though neither of them answered her phone calls.

Chapter 24

Myah decided to try to give Allen a call again, as she hoped that he would respond. First, she dialed his cell phone number, but there was no response. Then she tried his home phone number, but there was still no response. Afterward, Myah tried to call Albert, but there was no response from him either. Myah sighed as she hung the phone up. Then she went into Michael's room to check on him. He was still asleep. Just then, the phone rang. Myah walked over to it and answered it.

Hello?" Myah said.

"Hello, Myah. It's me, Endymion. I wanted to give you a call to see how you were doing."

"I still haven't heard from Allen or Albert."

"I've been searching for them. I haven't found a trace of either of them. I did see trails of blood, but I don't think that it came from either of them. I just don't understand it. I didn't see him anywhere. The only thing I can figure is that if they were responsible for what had happened, they probably tried to hide the evidence. They're probably not going to want to be found." Endymion said.

"I have a feeling you're not going to find him there."

"Something tells me you're right. I'm going to keep searching for the other two. I want answers. In the meantime, hang in there. I will return once I get to the bottom of this."

"Do you think that Allen and Albert may have gotten killed?" Myah asked.

"Let's not jump to conclusions. I realize that it looks bad, but there could be another explanation."

"It's not like Allen to not keep in touch. I fear that something may have happened to him."

"I will find answers. You have to believe that. I want you to try not to worry." Endymion said.

"It's kind of hard not to."

"I realize that, but being stressed out is not what you need, nor will it help you in any way. You've been under enough stress because of this. What I want you to do is take the day and try to relax and enjoy yourself. I realize that it's a difficult situation, but if you can, try to clear your mind. I will take care of it."

"What about the work that needs to be done? It's been a while since I've checked my emails."

"Myah, I understand, and there's no hurry. Please, try not to worry about it. Just leave everything to me." Endymion said.

"Okay, I'll try."

"I'll be in touch with you again soon to see how you're doing." Endymion said.

"Okay. Thank you."

"Take care of yourself, and I'll talk to you later." Endymion said.

They both said their goodbyes, and then Myah got off the phone and went to Michael's room to check on him again. That time, he was awake, so she took care of him, and then she spent time with him as she thought about what Endymion had told her.

Chapter 25

Myah decided to take Endymion's advice and take the day to relax. Since Michael was about to fall asleep, she put him into his crib. She smiled as she watched him as he drifted off to sleep. Myah sighed and then she left the room. As she entered the living room, she glanced out the window and noticed how pleasant the weather seemed. She thought it would be nice to step out for some fresh air. It was bright and sunny and the sky was clear. It had been several days since Myah had been outside. She was afraid to go out after she found out that Jayden was in the area. The last thing she wanted was for him to find her, even though she was relieved that he didn't die.

Even though she had not seen or heard anything from him for several days, Myah was still somewhat hesitant to leave her home, even though she wanted to go outside. She wasn't sure whether he may have still been in the area. Then again, it had been several days since he was last seen in the area. Myah glanced out the window, and then she glanced in the direction where Michael's room was. She decided to check on him to make sure he was still asleep, and he was alright. When she noticed that he was still asleep, she left the room, and then she got changed before she went outside. At first, Myah was nervous, but she wanted to enjoy the beautiful day. She glanced around for a moment, and then she got into the water, so she could go for a swim. The water was a bit chilly at first, but it didn't take long until she had gotten used to it, and it didn't seem as cold. Myah sighed, and then she looked around before she started to swim. The warmth of the sun felt good as Myah swam. She was happy that she was finally able to get outside and enjoy a nice swim on such a pleasant day. Everything seemed great until suddenly, Myah spotted someone standing on her porch, glancing around. Chills ran down Myah's spine as she got a good look at who it was. It was Jayden, and it was obvious that he was looking for her. Myah knew that she had to try to stay calm, even though tension continued to build up inside her. The last thing she wanted was to be trapped with Jayden as his prisoner once again. Myah took a deep breath and swam under the water as she hoped that he wouldn't spot her. She kept swimming until she had gotten to the boardwalk. She glanced around before she swam beneath the boardwalk, where she decided to hide from him. Myah's heart raced as she looked around. She hoped that Jayden would just go away so that she could go back inside. She wished she could've found another way back inside without being seen by Jayden. Myah wanted to get inside and lock every door and window, so he would have no way to get inside. Then she thought of the possibility of him going into her home, and she became even more afraid. Myah knew that once he got into her home, it would be very difficult to escape him. Myah looked around again and noticed how quiet everything seemed. It made her uncomfortable, even though it seemed like she had given him the slip. She glanced around again when, suddenly, she spotted Jayden beneath the boardwalk with her. He had an expression of anger on his face as he stared at her while he kept moving toward her. The expression on his face caused chills to run down Myah's spine. She acted quickly and splashed water in his face before she swam away. With an expression of fury on his face, Jayden followed her. Myah didn't know what to do because she knew that even if she had gotten inside, she would've never had enough time to lock every door and window before Jayden would get inside. As Myah continued to swim away from Jayden, he continued to follow her. Then she thought for a moment before she stopped. When Jayden approached her, he was about to take hold of her when she splashed water in his face again. Then, without hesitation, Myah took a deep breath before she went under the water. She hoped that she had given him the slip once again. Myah swam deeper and deeper, and she started to worry about what she would do when she was no longer able to hold her breath. Suddenly, she noticed something peculiar, and she swam toward it. As she got closer, she realized that it was a wall of water. Myah kept moving toward it as she hoped that it would be a good hiding spot for her. When she approached it, she glanced around before she swam through it. After getting through the wall of water, Myah exhaled, and then she took a deep breath. She suddenly became confused as she glanced around. Right before her was an unusual structure like nothing she had ever seen before. She spotted a door, and she nervously walked over to it and knocked on it. Then she glanced around before she tried the knob. Much to her surprise, the door came right open. Myah was hesitant at first, but then she stepped inside. As she looked around, she realized that the mysterious place was a home that had been built underwater. Myah began to worry as she realized that she had broken into someone else's home.

"Hello?" Myah said.

There was no answer. It seemed that nobody was there.

Myah started to walk through the place until she suddenly spotted a set of stairs that went up to a trap door in the ceiling. Myah became curious, so she started up the steps. As she climbed the stairs, she noticed that the trap door had a lock on it, and she became even more curious about it. When she approached it, she unlocked the door and then pushed it open. She was surprised when she discovered that it led to Michael's room. She was even more surprised when she realized that the underwater structure was actually part of her home.

Without hesitation, Myah rushed over to Michael's crib, snatched him out of it, and then she carefully started back downstairs to the underwater shelter. She made sure to pull the trapdoor shut, and then she locked it so that no one could get inside.

Chapter 26

After Myah had gotten back down the stairs, she glanced around before she decided to continue her walk through the place. She found it peculiar as she looked around as she realized that it seemed as though it had been set up just for her and her family. There was a room set up for Michael. There was even a room set up for the ones that Myah was expecting. Myah was surprised at how beautiful the place looked.

Suddenly, Myah heard the sound of footsteps. She knew at that moment that Jayden had gotten inside the house.

Myah hoped that he wouldn't find out about the underwater shelter. She definitely didn't want to be stuck with him in a place like that. There would be no way of escaping him for sure.

Myah had no intention of going back up to the main house. She felt she was safer where she was at, as long as he would never find out about it. Then she started to think about Endymion, and she worried about what would happen if he were to show up while Jayden was there, especially knowing how jealous Jayden was of him in the past. She wasn't sure if it was a good idea to try to contact him, so she could warn him. She didn't want the two of them to end up getting into a fight. At that moment, Myah felt that it was probably best if Endymion stayed away for a while so no problems would arise.

Chapter 27

For several days, Myah heard the sound of footsteps. She knew that Jayden was still there, and he was most likely on the lookout for her and Michael. Myah hoped that he would never figure it out. She hoped that he would eventually get tired of waiting and then leave. Myah also wished that she could've contacted Endymion, but she was afraid to at that point.

After a while, Myah heard the footsteps less often, and she wondered if Jayden was leaving off and on. Eventually, she didn't hear them at all but she was still afraid to leave her home.

Many more days had passed, and Myah had not heard a sound from upstairs. She wished she could've gone outside for a swim. As she thought about it, she wondered if an evening swim would be better.

Myah kept busy throughout the day with tidying up the house and taking care of Michael. Then she decided to check her emails. She noticed that there was a message from Endymion. She opened it and read it. He was checking to see how she was doing. As she continued to read the message, she realized that it seemed as though he knew something was up. She became nervous as she continued to read the message, and she realized that he was planning to stop over in a few days. He also mentioned in the message that she did not need to worry. She was still worried because she knew that if he showed up and Jayden was still around, it would be trouble. On the other hand,

Myah had not heard anything for a while, and she was hoping that it meant that Jayden had left. The last thing she wanted was even more trouble.

Chapter 28

Several hours had passed, and it was late in the evening, and Myah had just put Michael into his crib as he was about to fall asleep. She wished all the more that she could've gone swimming, but she wasn't sure about whether it was a good idea, even though she had not heard anything. As Myah thought about it, she wondered about whether it really would've been better to go out during the evening, so she'd be less likely to be seen. Since Michael had fallen asleep, she decided to go for an evening swim. She checked on him again before she got ready, and then she headed out through the secret door of her secret place. Myah held her breath as she swam up from under the water. She then exhaled before she took a deep breath and released it before she looked around. It was a clear evening with the moon shining down, reflecting onto the water. Everything seemed calm at that moment. As Myah looked at the reflection of the moonlight, she suddenly found herself trapped in a strong embrace. Myah knew right away that it was Jayden, and she struggled as she tried to break free from him. Suddenly, she found herself freed from his embrace. Myah became puzzled as she glanced around. Jayden was nowhere to be found. It was as though he had vanished from the area. Myah glanced around, and then she sighed as the coast seemed to be clear. She decided that it was best to head back inside, where it was safe. Myah took a deep breath before she started to swim toward her secret place. When she approached it, she was about to swim through the wall of water when she noticed something suspicious on the other side. Myah was about to swim away when Jayden suddenly came through the wall of water. Before Myah had a chance to swim away, Jayden took hold of her, pulled her toward the wall of water, and took her through it.

Chapter 29

Myah tried to break free from Jayden, but it was no use. He refused to let her go, even as she struggled to get freed from him. Jayden remained quiet as he kept Myah close to him as he opened the door, and then he took her inside. He let her go for a moment as he closed the door and locked it. Myah glanced toward Michael's room before she looked in the direction of where the stairs were. Then she glanced at Jayden before she looked toward the trap door again. She was about to rush toward it when Jayden quickly took hold of her. Then he pulled her toward him, and he held her tightly as he spoke into her ear.

"Not this time." Jayden said.

Myah tried to get herself freed from him.

"Let me go." she said.

"No. I'll never let you go." Jayden said.

Myah continued to struggle.

"Stop!" Jayden said.

Then suddenly, he let go of Myah, who rushed toward the stairs where the trapdoor was. Jayden then went after her. When Myah approached the stairs, she turned and glanced at Jayden before she started to climb up the steps. Then Jayden took hold of her and pulled her toward him.

"It'll do you no good. I knew you would try to escape, so I blocked it, so you couldn't get up there." Jayden said.

Once again, Myah found herself trying to get free from Jayden.

"You can't escape me, Myah! You might as well give up!" Jayden said.

Myah refused to give up. As she struggled to get free, Jayden let out a holler before he let her go. Myah took off running through the room, with Jayden chasing her. She headed for her bedroom as she hoped that she could get into the room before he captured her. She hoped that she would be able to barricade the door, so Jayden couldn't get into the room. When Myah approached the room, she quickly went into it and then closed the door. Myah glanced around as she hoped that she could find something to block the door shut, so Jayden couldn't get into the room. Just then, he started to pound on the door.

"Myah! Let me in!" Jayden said.

Myah wasn't sure how long she would be able to keep him out. He was determined to get into the room, which was the last thing that Myah wanted. She knew that the moment Jayden would get into the room, she'd have a more difficult time escaping him.

Myah continued to keep the door pushed shut, even though it was becoming more difficult. Just then, Jayden managed to push his way through, and he got into the room. It was then that Myah realized that there was no escape for her. Jayden closed the door, and then he looked at Myah before he moved toward her.

"Are you finished now?" Jayden asked.

Myah didn't respond.

"You probably thought I wouldn't figure it out, but the funny thing is, I knew about this the whole time. I never left because I knew that you were down here. That was why I blocked the trap door. Now, I have you right where I want you. I was waiting for the right moment to make my move. That moment has come.” Jayden said.

Myah continued to back away from Jayden, who looked at her angrily.

“Stop trying to escape me! I’ve had enough of this! It’s time to put an end to it!” Jayden said.

“What are you going to do?” Myah asked.

“I’m going to make sure you never escape me again.”

“Please, don’t.”

“I told you to stop hurting me, yet you wouldn’t stop.”

“It’s not my fault.” Myah said.

“Of course not. It never is.”

“What’s that supposed to mean?”

"You wouldn't stop running from me, even after I asked you to stop."

"You didn't ask me, Jayden, you were yelling at me, and you even threatened me." Myah said.

When Jayden approached her, he took hold of her and held her tightly. Myah tried to escape him, but it was no use.

"Enough! This ends now!" Jayden said.

"Please, let me go."

"No."

"Why? I didn't ask for this."

"Because even now, you wish to escape me."

"It's because you're scaring me."

"Oh, so now I'm scary. How do you think I felt whenever your brother gunned me down?" Jayden said.

Myah stopped struggling, and then she glanced at Jayden, who had a stern expression on his face.

"Let me guess. You don't believe me." Jayden said.

Myah said nothing as she looked away from him. With an expression of fury on his face, Jayden let Myah go, and then she looked at Jayden, who started unbuttoning his shirt. Then Myah closed her eyes and looked away.

"Is this proof enough for you, Myah! Is it real enough for you!" Jayden said.

Myah kept her eyes closed as refused to look at him.

"Look at me!" Jayden said.

Myah's eyes filled with tears as she looked at Jayden. She broke down and cried when she noticed the bullet wounds on his chest and abdomen.

"He tried to kill me, Myah. Can't you see that? He didn't just shoot me once, no, he shot me twice. Also, have you noticed where he shot me? I can promise you that it was deliberate, and it was with intent to murder me." Jayden said.

Tears ran down Myah's face as she looked at Jayden's wounds, and then she looked into his eyes that were full of hurt.

"I had no weapon, I was defenseless. He and Albert both ganged up on me, and they beat me before Allen shot me. I could've taken them down, but you see, I had no intention of fighting them. I just wanted to get to you, but they weren't having it. To make things worse, they thought I was dead, so they decided to carry me off and throw me into a ravine." Jayden said.

Myah said nothing as she looked at him with her tear-filled eyes.

"What they did was no accident, Myah. As I said, Allen did it with the intent to kill me. He was the one person who kept getting between you and me. He took it too far." Jayden said.

Myah looked at the wounds again as they bled.

"It hurts. The bullets are still there." Jayden said.

"Why didn't you go to the hospital?"

"Because I just can't. Besides, I wanted to find you. I wanted to be with you."

"Jayden, you need help."

"I know. I need you to take care of me. You owe me that since your brother tried to kill me." Jayden said.

"What do you want me to do?" Myah asked.

"I already told you that I want you to take care of me. That's the least you could do for me."

"I can't." Myah said.

"I need you to listen to me. I need you to do something for me."

"What is it?" Myah asked.

"As I told you before, the bullets are still inside me. I need you to take them out."

"No."

"No is not an option, Myah. I need you to do this for me."

"I can't."

"Why not?"

"Because I'm afraid I'll hurt you."

"I'm already hurting."

"No, Jayden. I can't do it. You need to go to the hospital."

"No, I want you to do this for me." Jayden said.

He then took hold of Myah's arm, and he took her over to the bed. Jayden got out of his wet clothes before he took hold of Myah's hands.

"I need you to do this for me. You can't run out on me like you always do." Jayden said.

"I wish you'd just go to the hospital."

"No."

"Why?"

"Because this is where I want to be."

“But you could die.”

“As if you even care.” Jayden said.

Myah’s eyes welled up with tears as she watched Jayden as he laid down on the bed.

“I could probably press charges against your brother. He knew exactly what he was doing. If you haven’t heard from him, it’s probably because he’s hiding. Albert would be in trouble as well. He’s your brother’s accomplice. Did you know that he was planning to kill me?” Jayden said.

“No, I can honestly say that I had no idea that he was planning to do that.”

“The real question is, can I believe you?”

“Jayden, I didn’t know that he was planning to shoot you. Had I known that, I would’ve never left.”

"Right, well, you shouldn't have left anyway." Jayden said.

"I'm sorry." Myah said.

"Well, as I said, I could press charges, and perhaps I will. It would be life in prison for both of them, perhaps even the death sentence for one of them. Of course, there may be a possibility of me overlooking the matter under one condition."

"What would that be?" Myah asked.

"I may forget the entire thing if you promise to stay with me forever. No more running, and no more mind games. What will it be, Myah? Will you spend your life with me? Or will your brother spend his life behind bars?" Jayden said.

"Okay. No more running. I promise." Myah said.

Jayden sat up on the bed, and then he took hold of both of Myah's hands as he looked into her eyes.

"Do you truly mean that?" Jayden asked.

Myah kept her eyes on his as she spoke.

"Yes, Jayden. I do." she said.

"Thank you. Now, please, help me. You know what you need to do. I know you can do it." Jayden said.

He kissed her hands before he laid back down. Myah looked at Jayden nervously, and she hesitated for a moment before she tried to take the bullet out of the wound in his abdomen. Myah tried to remain calm, although it was difficult since she was uncomfortable about what she was doing.

After the bullet was removed from the wound in Jayden's abdomen, Myah looked at the wound that was on his chest. Tears ran down her face as she looked into his eyes.

"I can't do this." Myah said.

"You had gotten the other one out. You can't stop now."

"Please, let me take you to the hospital."

"No, Myah. I need you to do this." Jayden said.

With tears streaming down her face, Myah carefully worked on removing the remaining bullet from the wound that was in Jayden's chest. She was finding it increasingly difficult to remain calm, as she continued to try to remove the bullet. After working diligently on it, Myah managed to remove it, but Jayden started to bleed more than he already was.

"Jayden, you need help." Myah said.

"No, I need you."

"Let me take you to the hospital."

"No. I need you to hold me."

"You're going to die."

"Myah?"

"Yes?"

"I'm glad that you've chosen not to run anymore." Jayden said.

Myah started to cry as she saw blood running from Jayden's wounds.

"Don't be upset, my dear. It's a win-win for everyone. We get to be together as a family, as it should be, and Allen and Albert get to stay out of prison." Jayden said.

"Jayden, you need to listen to me. You need to go to the hospital. You're going to end up bleeding to death."

"I've been through worse."

"How? You've been shot in the chest. It's a wonder you're not dead already."

"You need to try to remain calm."

"Just stop. You're not taking me seriously. I can't do this. I just can't deal with this. I can't handle the thought of you…"

"What." Jayden said.

"I can't handle the thought of you dying." Myah said.

Jayden reached up and touched the side of Myah's face.

"Do you really think I had any idea about what they were planning to do? I didn't. I'm so disappointed in Allen for what he did. I never wanted that. I knew that something had gone wrong that day, and when I had received those packages, and that envelope…" Myah said.

At that moment, she broke down and wept.

"When I thought that you had died, it devastated me." Myah said.

"Then stop running from me."

"I told you that I would." Myah said.

Tears ran down her face as she looked into Jayden's eyes.

"The truth is, I never stopped caring about you, in fact, I've never felt the way I feel about anyone, except you."

"Then give me what I want." Jayden said.

"I don't want to lose you, not again."

“You won't.”

“I'm so afraid that you're going to die.”

“I'll be alright. Just hold me. Hold me like you never held me before. Do it as though both of our lives depended on it.” Jayden said.

Myah took Jayden in her arms and held him tightly as she broke down and cried.

“I'm so sorry, for everything. I'm sorry that I refused to believe you. The truth is, you were right. Deep down, I knew it, but I was in denial because I was running from it. I was running from the truth. I wish I could take it back. He really does look like you. He's beautiful, just like you.” Myah said.

“Myah?”

“Yes?”

“Kiss me.” Jayden said.

Myah closed her eyes as she gave Jayden a kiss. Then they both looked into each other's eyes as Jayden spoke.

"I'm right where I want to be at this moment. I wouldn't have it any other way because it's as it should be. If for some reason I wouldn't pull through this, at least I can be content knowing that I'd be spending my last moments just as I'd want to spend them."

"No, Jayden. You can't do this to me. You can't leave me."

"Myah? I love you." Jayden said.

"Please, don't do this." Myah said.

Jayden gazed into Myah's eyes as he reached up to touch her face. Suddenly, his eyes closed and he became unconscious.

"Jayden? Jayden?" Myah said.

Jayden didn't respond.

"Please, don't go. I need you. Michael needs you. Also, I didn't lose the baby, in fact, there are two of them. They need you." Myah said.

Tears ran down her face as she took hold of Jayden's hand.

"Jayden, I love you." Myah said.

She kissed him, and she suddenly felt his hand squeeze hers. It was as though he was letting her know that he could still hear her. Myah hugged him tightly as she wept, as she feared that it would soon be the end for him.

Chapter 30

As Myah sat on the bed, she became more uncomfortable with the situation that she was in. She knew that Jayden needed help but for some reason, he didn't want to go to the hospital. Myah knew that she had to do something. She couldn't just let him die. Unfortunately, Jayden's condition was critical, and it was worsening. Myah feared the possibility of it already being too late for him. Myah looked at Jayden's face before she tried to move from where she was sitting. She was careful as she managed to get up, and then she rushed over to the phone and dialed the emergency number. It wasn't long until someone picked it up. Myah was confused when she heard the voice on the other end.

"Hello?" Endymion said.

"Endymion?" Myah said.

"Yes, Myah. Is there something wrong?"

"Yes, I must have dialed the wrong number."

"No, you haven't. Talk to me."

"I can't. I don't have time."

"Myah, listen to me. I want to help you."

"Please. He's here, and he's dying. It may already be too late for him."

"I'm coming over." Endymion said.

"Wait! You won't know where to find us. We're not in the main house." Myah said.

There was no response. She then realized that Endymion was no longer on the other end. Myah became frustrated. She was about to dial the emergency number when suddenly, she heard something.

"Myah."

Myah turned, and she saw Endymion standing in the room.

"But how did you know?" Myah asked.

"Never mind that. We don't have time for that. We need to focus on what's important." Endymion said.

He then walked over to the bed where Jayden was laying. His eyes filled with tears as he looked at him.

"He's in very bad shape, but I can help him." Endymion said.

He sighed before he sat down at Jayden's bedside. He glanced at Myah before he put his hands on Jayden's wounds. Endymion kept his hands on the wounds until they had fully healed. Then he caused Jayden to remain asleep. Endymion broke down in tears as he hugged Jayden, who remained asleep. He was relieved that he had not died. Endymion then glanced at Myah before he spoke.

"He should be fine now. I caused him to remain asleep. Don't be alarmed. It's not permanent. He's exhausted and needs to rest." Endymion said.

"I want to thank you for what you did for him. You have no idea how much it means to me. You saved his life." Myah said.

"I'm just thankful that he's alive. It was painful to think that he wasn't and I hated the very thought of having to lay him to rest." Endymion said.

Myah then walked over to the bed, sat down, and then she took Jayden in her arms even as he slept. Endymion's eyes welled up with tears as he looked at Jayden, who remained asleep.

"He came so close to death. It's a wonder he made it this far." Endymion said.

"He didn't want me to call for help."

"Had you not called for help, he would've died. He was bleeding internally, and he had lost a lot of blood even before he came here."

"He wouldn't listen to me, even though I told him that he needed help. He just wanted me to hold him."

"You did the right thing by calling me. Had you not made that call, he would've died in your arms. You have no idea how close to death he truly was." Endymion said.

As he closed his eyes, a tear trickled down his face.

"Do you love him?" Endymion asked.

"Yes."

"Are you sure?"

"Yes."

"You must know that you're going to have your hands full with him. I sincerely hope that you're going to be prepared for that."

"I realize that he's an emotional mess, but I promised to never run from him again." Myah said.

She could tell by the look on Endymion's face that his concern was growing by the second.

"Myah, he's a very broken man. There are things that I know that I have a feeling that you don't know. Unfortunately, it's not my place to tell you about those things. It's his."

"I can't help but notice the striking resemblance between the two of you. Your hair, skin, and eye color are different from his, but aside from that, you look alike." Myah said.

Endymion had no response as he looked at her.

"I realize that he can be a bit difficult to deal with, but he's Michael's father. He's also the father of the ones that I'm carrying." Myah said.

"I understand that. I'm just asking you to be careful."

"I will, and I appreciate how much you care, but my mind has been made up. I'm never going to leave him because I realized that I'm even more miserable without him." Myah said.

Endymion watched Myah closely as she ran her fingers through Jayden's hair.

"The truth is, I love him so much. I've never felt this way about anyone before. There was only one other person who I've ever had feelings for, but that was just a silly crush." Myah said.

She then closed her eyes as she gave Jayden a kiss. Endymion had a sorrowful expression on his face as he looked at both of them.

"Very well, however, I will continue to check up on you to see how you're doing and make sure everything is okay. If you need anything, don't be afraid to give me a call." Endymion said.

He was about to leave when he glanced at Myah before he spoke.

"There's just one more thing. Don't tell him that I was here. You may be wondering why I'm asking this of you, but trust me, it's for the best." Endymion said.

He then left Myah's underwater shelter.

Chapter 31

It was early in the morning when Jayden woke up. He was suddenly confused because he realized that the pain he had felt was gone. Jayden put his hand on his chest and he realized that the bullet wound was no longer there. Then he touched his abdomen where the other wound used to be, and he realized that it was also gone. Jayden was perplexed because he had no idea how he was able to heal as quickly as he did. He was aware of how severe his condition once was, and he knew that his chance of survival was once slim. Jayden glanced over at Myah, who was still asleep. He continued to think about how close he was to death before he had healed. Jayden then sighed, and then he closed his eyes as he gave Myah a kiss. He opened his eyes and looked at her before he gave her another kiss as he hoped to wake her up. Jayden looked at her again before he gave her another kiss. He wouldn't stop until Myah had woken up. She opened her eyes and looked at Jayden, who gave her another kiss. Myah sat up and then Jayden moved closer to her before he snuggled up to her. She hugged him tightly because she was relieved that he would be alright. Jayden then looked into Myah's eyes as he rested against her.

"Is it true?" Jayden asked.

"What?"

"You told me something, or at least, I think you did. Maybe it was all just a dream. It was something regarding the pregnancy."

"I did tell you something."

"Did I hear you correctly?"

"What did you hear?" Myah asked.

She ran her fingers through his hair as they looked into each other's eyes.

"You told me that you didn't lose the baby and that there are actually two of them. Is it true?"

"Yes. It's true." Myah said.

Jayden's eyes lit up, and he sat up as he kept his eyes on Myah's eyes. Then he showered her with kisses because he was happy about what he had heard. Then he looked into her eyes again before he kissed her abdomen.

"You have no idea how happy it makes me to know that we haven't lost the baby. It makes me even happier to know that there are two of them. I just want you to know that I'm very sorry for what I have done. I promise that it will never happen again." Jayden said.

He then smiled, and he closed his eyes as he put his forehead against Myah's as he spoke.

"It looks like it's a new beginning for us. This time, there will be nothing standing in our way. We will finally have the life we were meant to have together."

www.ingramcontent.com/pod-product-compliance
Lightning Source LLC
Chambersburg PA
CBHW072229150726
48002CB00005B/2002